IT TAKES A THIEF

IT TAKES A THIEF

by Walter Miller, Jr.

Strange gods were worshiped on Mars. But were they so clever? They'd lost their own world.

"The ancient gods, our Fathers, rode down from the heavens in the Firebirds of the Sun. Coming into the world, they found no air for the breath of their souls. "How shall we breathe?" they asked of the Sun. And Sun gave them of His fire and beneath the earth they kindled the Blaze of the Great Wind. Good air roared from the womb of Mars our Mother, the ice burned with a great thunder, and there was air for the breath of Man."

—FROM AN OLD MARTIAN LEGEND

A thief, he was about to die like a thief.

He hung from the post by his wrists. The wan sunlight glistened faintly on his naked back as he waited, eyes tightly closed, lips moving slowly as he pressed his face against the rough wood and stood on tiptoe to relieve the growing ache in his shoulders. When his ankles ached, he hung by the nails that pierced his forearms just above the wrists.

He was young, perhaps in his tenth Marsyear, and his crisp black hair was close-cropped in the fashion of the bachelor who had not yet sired a pup, or not yet admitted that he had. Lithe and sleek, with the quick knotty muscles and slender rawhide limbs of a wild thing, half-fed and hungry with a quick furious hunger that crouched in ambush. His face, though twisted with pain and fright, remained that of a cocky pup.

When he opened his eyes he could see the low hills of Mars, sun-washed and gray-green with trees, trees brought down from the heavens by the Ancient Fathers. But he could also see the executioner in the foreground, sitting spraddle-legged and calm while he chewed a blade of grass and waited. A squat man with a thick face, he occasionally peered at the thief with empty blue eyes—while he casually played mumblety-peg with the bleeding-blade. His stare was blank.

"Are you ready for me, Asir?"

"Ready for me yet, Asir?" he grumbled, not unpleasantly.

5

IT TAKES A THIEF

The knifeman sat beyond spitting range, but Asir spat, and tried to wipe his chin on the post. "Your dirty mother!" he mumbled.

The executioner chuckled and played mumblety-peg.

After three hours of dangling from the spikes that pierced his arms, Asir was weakening, and the blood throbbed hard in his temples, with each jolt of his heart a separate pulse of pain. The red stickiness had stopped oozing down his arms; they knew how to drive the spike just right. But the heartbeats labored in his head like a hammer beating at red-hot iron.

How many heartbeats in a life-time—and how many left to him now?

He whimpered and writhed, beginning to lose all hope. Mara had gone to see the Chief Commoner, to plead with him for the pilferer's life—but Mara was about as trustworthy as a wild hüffen, and he had visions of them chuckling together in Tokra's villa over a glass of amber wine, while life drained slowly from a young thief.

Asir regretted nothing. His father had been a renegade before him, had squandered his last ritual formula to buy a wife, then impoverished, had taken her away to the hills. Asir was born in the hills, but he came back to the village of his ancestors to work as a servant and steal the rituals of his masters. No thief could last for long. A ritual-thief caused havoc in the community. The owner of a holy phrase, not knowing that it had been stolen, tried to spend it—and eventually counter-claims would come to light, and a general accounting had to be called. The thief was always found out.

Asir had stolen more than wealth, he had stolen the strength of their souls. For this they hung him by his wrists and waited for him to beg for the bleeding-blade.

Woman thirsts for husband,
Man thirsts for wife,
Baby thirsts for breast-milk
Thief thirsts for knife....

A rhyme from his childhood, a childish chant, an eenie-meenie-miney for determining who should drink first from a nectar-cactus. He groaned and tried to shift his weight more comfortably. Where was Mara?

*

"Ready for me yet, Asir?" the squat man asked.

Asir hated him with narrowed eyes. The executioner was bound by law to wait until his victim requested his fate. But Asir remained ignorant of what the fate would be. The Council of Senior Kinsmen judged him in secret, and passed sentence as to what the executioner would do with the knife. But Asir was not informed of their judgment. He knew only that when he asked for it, the executioner would advance with the bleeding-blade and exact the punishment—his life, or an amputation, depending on the judgment. He might lose only an eye or an ear or a finger. But on the other hand, he might lose his life, both arms, or his masculinity.

There was no way to find out until he asked for the punishment. If he refused to ask, they would leave him hanging there. In theory, a thief could escape by hanging four days, after which the executioner would pull out the nails. Sometimes a culprit managed it, but when the nails were pulled, the thing that toppled was already a corpse.

The sun was sinking in the west, and it blinded him. Asir knew about the sun—knew things the stupid council failed to know. A thief, if successful, frequently became endowed with wisdom, for he memorized more wealth than a score of honest men. Quotations from the ancient gods—Fermi, Einstein, Elgermann, Hanser and the rest—most men owned scattered phrases, and scattered phrases remained meaningless. But a thief memorized all transactions that he overheard, and the countless phrases could be fitted together into meaningful ideas.

He knew now that Mars, once dead, was dying again, its air leaking away once more into space. And Man would die with it, unless something were done, and done quickly. The Blaze of the Great Wind needed to be rekindled under the earth, but it would not be done. The tribes had fallen into ignorance, even as the holy books had warned:

It is realized that the colonists will be unable to maintain a technology without basic tools, and that a rebuilding will require several generations of intelligently directed effort. Given the knowledge, the colonists may be able to restore a machine culture if the knowledge continues to be bolstered by desire. But if the third, fourth, and Nth generations fail to further the gradual retooling process, the knowledge will become worthless.

The quotation was from the god Roggins, *Progress of the Mars-Culture*, and he had stolen bits of it from various sources. The books themselves were no longer in existence, remembered only in memorized ritual chants, the possession of which meant wealth.

Asir was sick. Pain and slow loss of blood made him weak, and his vision blurred. He failed to see her coming until he heard her feet rustling in the dry grass.

"Mara—"

She smirked and spat contemptuously at the foot of the post. The daughter of a Senior Kinsman, she was a tall, slender girl with an arrogant strut and mocking eyes. She stood for a moment with folded arms, eyeing him with amusement. Then, slowly, one eye closed in a solemn wink. She turned her back on him and spoke to the executioner.

"May I taunt the prisoner, Slubil?" she asked.

"It is forbidden to speak to the thief," growled the knifeman.

"Is he ready to beg for justice, Slubil?"

The knifeman grinned and looked at Asir. "Are you ready for me yet, thief?"

Asir hissed an insult. The girl had betrayed him.

"Evidently a coward," she said. "Perhaps he means to hang four days."

"Let him then."

"No—I think that I should *like* to see him beg."

She gave Asir a long searching glance, then turned to walk away. The thief cursed her quietly and followed her with his eyes. A dozen steps away she stopped again, looked back over her shoulder, and repeated the slow wink. Then she marched on toward her father's house. The wink made his scalp crawl for a moment, but then....

Suppose she hasn't betrayed me? Suppose she had wheedled the sentence out of Tokra, and knew what his punishment would be. *I think that I should like to see him beg.*

But on the other hand, the fickle she-devil might be tricking him into asking for a sentence that she *knew* would be death or dismemberment—just to amuse herself.

He cursed inwardly and trembled as he peered at the bored executioner. He licked his lips and fought against dizzyness as he groped for words. Slubil heard him muttering and looked up.

"Are you ready for me yet?"

*

Asir closed his eyes and gritted his teeth. "Give it to me!" he yelped suddenly, and braced himself against the post.

Why not? The short time gained couldn't be classed as living. Have it done with. Eternity would be sweet in comparison to this ignomy. A knife could be a blessing.

He heard the executioner chuckle and stand up. He heard the man's footsteps approaching slowly, and the singing hiss of the knife as Slubil swung it in quick arcs. The executioner moved about him slowly, teasing him with the whistle of steel fanning the air about him. He was expected to beg. Slubil occasionally laid the knife against his skin and took it away again. Then Asir heard the rustle of the executioner's cloak as his arm went back. Asir opened his eyes.

The executioner grinned as he held the blade high—aimed at Asir's head! The girl had tricked him. He groaned and closed his eyes again, muttering a half-forgotten prayer.

The stroke fell—and the blade chopped into the post above his head. Asir fainted.

When he awoke he lay in a crumpled heap on the ground. The executioner rolled him over with his foot.

"In view of your extreme youth, thief," the knifeman growled, "the council has ordered you perpetually banished. The sun is setting. Let dawn find you

9

in the hills. If you return to the plains, you will be chained to a wild hüffen and dragged to death."

Panting weakly, Asir groped at his forehead, and found a fresh wound, raw and rubbed with rust to make a scar. Slubil had marked him as an outcast. But except for the nail-holes through his forearms, he was still in one piece. His hands were numb, and he could scarcely move his fingers. Slubil had bound the spike-wounds, but the bandages were bloody and leaking.

When the knifeman had gone, Asir climbed weakly to his feet. Several of the townspeople stood nearby, snickering at him. He ignored their catcalls and staggered toward the outskirts of the village, ten minutes away. He had to speak to Mara, and to her father if the crusty oldster would listen. His thief's knowledge weighed upon him and brought desperate fear.

Darkness had fallen by the time he came to Welkir's house. The people spat at him in the streets, and some of them flung handfuls of loose dirt after him as he passed. A light flickered feebly through Welkir's door. Asir rattled it and waited.

Welkir came with a lamp. He set the lamp on the floor and stood with feet spread apart, arms folded, glaring haughtily at the thief. His face was stiff as weathered stone. He said nothing, but only stared contemptuously.

Asir bowed his head. "I have come to plead with you, Senior Kinsman."

Welkir snorted disgust. "Against the mercy we have shown you?"

He looked up quickly, shaking his head. "No! For that I am grateful."

"What then?"

"As a thief, I acquired much wisdom. I know that the world is dying, and the air is boiling out of it into the sky. I wish to be heard by the council. We must study the words of the ancients and perform their magic, lest our children's children be born to strangle in a dead world."

Welkir snorted again. He picked up the lamp. "He who listens to a thief's wisdom is cursed. He who acts upon it is doubly cursed and a party to the crime."

"The vaults," Asir insisted. "The key to the Blaze of the Winds is in the vaults. The god Roggins tells us in the words—"

"Stop! I will not hear!"

"Very well, but the blaze can be rekindled, and the air renewed. The vaults—" He stammered and shook his head. "The council must hear me."

"The council will hear nothing, and you shall be gone before dawn. And the vaults are guarded by the sleeper called Big Joe. To enter is to die. Now go away."

*

Welkir stepped back and slammed the door. Asir sagged in defeat. He sank down on the doorstep to rest a moment. The night was black, except for lamp-flickers from an occasional window.

"Ssssst!"

A sound from the shadows. He looked around quickly, searching for the source.

"Ssssst! Asir!"

It was the girl Mara, Welkir's daughter. She had slipped out the back of the house and was peering at him around the corner. He arose quietly and went to her.

"What did Slubil do to you?" she whispered.

Asir gasped and caught her shoulders angrily. "Don't you *know*?"

"No! Stop! You're hurting me. Tokra wouldn't tell me. I made love to him, but he wouldn't tell."

He released her with an angry curse.

"You *had* to take it sometime," she hissed. "I knew if you waited you would be too weak from hanging to even run away."

He called her a foul name.

"Ingrate!" she snapped. "And I bought you a hüffen!"

"You *what*?"

"Tokra gave me a ritual phrase and I bought you a hüffen with it. You can't *walk* to the hills, you know."

Asir burned with dull rage. "You slept with Tokra!" he snapped.

"You're jealous!" she tittered.

"How can I be jealous! I hate the sight of you!"

11

"Very well then, I'll keep the hüffen."

"*Do!*" he growled. "I won't need it, since I'm not going to the hills!"

She gasped. "You've got to go, you fool! They'll kill you!"

He turned away, feeling sick. She caught at his arm and tried to pull him back. "Asir! Take the hüffen and *go!*"

"I'll go," he growled. "But not to the hills. I'm going out to the vault."

He stalked away, but she trotted along beside him, trying to tug him back. "Fool! The vaults are sacred! The priests guard the entrance, and the Sleeper guards the inner door. They'll kill you if you try it, and if you linger, the council will kill you tomorrow."

"Let them!" he snarled. "I am no sniveling townsman! I am of the hills, and my father was a renegade. Your council had no right to judge me. Now *I* shall judge *them.*"

The words were spoken hotly, and he realized their folly. He expected a scornful rebuke from Mara, but she hung onto his arm and pleaded with him. He had dragged her a dozen doorways from the house of her father. Her voice had lost its arrogance and became pleading.

"Please, Asir! Go away. Listen! I will even go with you—if you want me."

He laughed harshly. "Tokra's leavings."

She slapped him hard across the mouth. "Tokra is an impotent old dodderer. He can scarcely move for arthritis. You're an idiot! I sat on his lap and kissed his bald pate for you."

"Then why did he give you a ritual phrase?" he asked stiffly.

"Because he likes me."

"You lie." He stalked angrily on.

"Very well! Go to the vaults. I'll tell my father, and they'll hunt you down before you get there."

She released his arm and stopped. Asir hesitated. She meant it. He came back to her slowly, then slipped his swollen hands to her throat. She did not back away.

"Why don't I just choke you and leave you lying here?" he hissed.

Her face was only a shadow in darkness, but he could see her cool smirk.

"Because you love me, Asir of Franic."

He dropped his hands and grunted a low curse. She laughed low and took his arm.

"Come on. We'll go get the hüffen," she said.

Why not? he thought. *Take her hüffen, and take her too.* He could dump her a few miles from the village, then circle back to the vaults. She leaned against him as they moved back toward her father's house, then skirted it and stole back to the field behind the row of dwellings. Phobos hung low in the west, its tiny disk lending only a faint glow to the darkness.

He heard the hüffen's breathing as they approached a hulking shadow in the gloom. Its great wings snaked out slowly as it sensed their approach, and it made a low piping sound. A native Martian species, it bore no resemblance to the beasts that the ancients had brought with them from the sky. Its back was covered with a thin shell like a beetle's, but its belly was porous and soft. It digested food by sitting on it, and absorbing it. The wings were bony—parchment stretched across a fragile frame. It was headless, and lacked a centralized brain, the nervous functions being distributed.

*

The great creature made no protest as they climbed up the broad flat back and strapped themselves down with the belts that had been threaded through holes cut in the hüffen's thin, tough shell. It's lungs slowly gathered a tremendous breath of air, causing the riders to rise up as the huge air-sacs became distended. The girth of an inflated hüffen was nearly four times as great as when deflated. When the air was gathered, the creature began to shrink again as its muscles tightened, compressing the breath until a faint leakage-hiss came from behind. It waited, wings taut.

The girl tugged at a ring set through the flesh of its flank. There was a blast of sound and a jerk. Nature's experiment in jet propulsion soared ahead and turned into the wind. Its first breath exhausted, it gathered another and blew itself ahead again. The ride was jerky. Each tailward belch was a rough lurch. They let the hüffen choose its own heading as it gained altitude. Then Mara tugged at the wing-straps, and the creature wheeled to soar toward the dark hills in the distance.

Asir sat behind her, a sardonic smirk on his face, as the wind whipped about them. He waited until they had flown beyond screaming distance of the village. Then he took her shoulders lightly in his hands. Mistaking it for affection, she leaned back against him easily and rested her dark head on his shoulder. He kissed her—while his hand felt gingerly for the knife at her belt. His fingers were numb, but he managed to clutch it, and press the blade lightly against her throat. She gasped. With his other hand, he caught her hair.

"Now guide the hüffen down!" he ordered.

"*Asir!*"

"Quickly!" he barked.

"What are you going to do?"

"Leave you here and circle back to the vaults."

"No! Not out here at night!"

He hesitated. There were slinking prowlers on the Cimmerian plain, beasts who would regard the marooned daughter of Welkir a delicious bit of good fortune, a gustatory delight of a sort they seldom were able to enjoy. Even above the moan of the wind, he could hear an occasional howl-cry from the fanged welcoming committee that waited for its dinner beneath them.

"Very well," he growled reluctantly. "Turn toward the vaults. But one scream and I'll slice you." He took the blade from her throat but kept the point touching her back.

"Please, Asir, *no!*" she pleaded. "Let me go on to the hills. Why do you want to go to the vaults? Because of Tokra?"

He gouged her with the point until she yelped. "Tokra be damned, and you with him!" he snarled. "Turn back."

"*Why?*"

"I'm going down to kindle the Blaze of the Winds."

"You're *mad!* The spirits of the ancients live in the vaults."

"I am going to kindle the Blaze of the Winds," he insisted stubbornly. "Now either turn back, or go down and I'll turn back alone."

*

After a hesitant moment, she tugged at a wing-rein and the hüffen banked majestically. They flew a mile to the south of the village, then beyond it toward the cloister where the priests of Big Joe guarded the entrance to the vaults. The cloister was marked by a patch of faint light on the ground ahead.

"Circle around it once," he ordered.

"You can't get in. They'll kill you."

He doubted it. No one ever tried to enter, except the priests who carried small animals down as sacrifices to the great Sleeper. Since no outsider ever dared go near the shaft, the guards expected no one. He doubted that they would be alert.

The cloister was a hollow square with a small stone tower rising in the center of the courtyard. The tower contained the entrance to the shaft. In the dim light of Phobos, assisted by yellow flickers from the cloister windows, he peered at the courtyard as they circled closer. It seemed to be empty.

"Land beside the tower!" he ordered.

"Asir—please—"

"Do it!"

The hüffen plunged rapidly, soared across the outer walls, and burst into the courtyard. It landed with a rough jolt and began squeaking plaintively.

"Hurry!" he hissed. "Get your straps off and let's go."

"I'm not going."

A prick of the knife point changed her mind. They slid quickly to the ground, and Asir kicked the hüffen in the flanks. The beast sucked in air and burst aloft.

Startled faces were trying to peer through the lighted cloister windows into the courtyard. Someone cried a challenge. Asir darted to the door of the tower and dragged it open. Now forced to share the danger, the girl came with him without urging. They stepped into a stair-landing. A candle flickered from a wall bracket. A guard, sitting on the floor beneath the

15

candle, glanced up in complete surprise. Then he reached for a short barbed pike. Asir kicked him hard in the temple, then rolled his limp form outside. Men with torches were running across the courtyard. He slammed the heavy metal door and bolted it.

Fists began beating on the door. They paused for a moment to rest, and Mara stared at him in fright. He expected her to burst into angry speech, but she only leaned against the wall and panted. The dark mouth of the stairway yawned at them—a stone throat that led into the bowels of Mars and the realm of the monster, Big Joe. He glanced at Mara thoughtfully, and felt sorry for her.

"I can leave you here," he offered, "but I'll have to tie you."

She moistened her lips, glanced first at the stairs, then at the door where the guards were raising a frantic howl. She shook her head.

"I'll go with you."

"The priests won't bother you, if they see that you were a prisoner."

"I'll go with you."

He was pleased, but angry with himself for the pleasure. An arrogant, spiteful, conniving wench, he told himself. She'd lied about Tokra. He grunted gruffly, seized the candle, and started down the stairs. When she started after him, he stiffened and glanced back, remembering the barbed pike.

As he had suspected, she had picked it up. The point was a foot from the small of his back. They stared at each other, and she wore her self-assured smirk.

"Here," she said, and handed it casually. "You might need this."

*

They stared at each other again, but it was different this time. Bewildered, he shook his head and resumed the descent toward the vaults. The guards were battering at the door behind them.

The stairwell was damp and cold. Blackness folded about them like a shroud. They moved in silence, and after five thousand steps, Asir stopped counting.

Somewhere in the depths, Big Joe slept his restless sleep. Asir wondered grimly how long it would take the guards to tear down the metal door. Somehow they had to get past Big Joe before the guards came thundering after them. There was a way to get around the monster: of that he was certain. A series of twenty-four numbers was involved, and he had memorized them with a stolen bit of ritual. How to use them was a different matter. He imagined vaguely that one must call them out in a loud voice before the inner entrance.

The girl walked beside him now, and he could feel her shivering. His eyes were quick and nervous as he scanned each pool of darkness, each nook and cranny along the stairway wall. The well was silent except for the mutter of their footsteps, and the gloom was full of musty odors. The candle afforded little light.

"I told you the truth about Tokra," she blurted suddenly.

Asir glowered straight ahead and said nothing, embarrassed by his previous jealousy. They moved on in silence.

Suddenly she stopped. "Look," she hissed, pointing down ahead.

He shielded the candle with his hand and peered downward toward a small square of dim light. "The bottom of the stairs," he muttered.

The light seemed faint and diffuse, with a slight greenish cast. Asir blew out the candle, and the girl quickly protested.

"How will we see to climb again?"

He laughed humorlessly. "What makes you think we will?"

She moaned and clutched at his arm, but came with him as he descended slowly toward the light. The stairway opened into a long corridor whose ceiling was faintly luminous. White-faced and frightened, they paused on the bottom step and looked down the corridor. Mara gasped and covered her eyes.

"Big Joe!" she whispered in awe.

He stared through the stairwell door and down the corridor through another door into a large room. Big Joe sat in the center of the room, sleeping his sleep of ages amid a heap of broken and whitening bones. A creature of metal, twice the height of Asir, he had obviously been designed to kill. Tri-fingered hands with gleaming talons, and a monstrous head shaped like a Marswolf, with long silver fangs. Why should a metal-creature have fangs, unless he had been built to kill?

The behemoth slept in a crouch, waiting for the intruders.

He tugged the girl through the stairwell door. A voice droned out of nowhere: "*If you have come to plunder, go back!*"

He stiffened, looking around. The girl whimpered.

"Stay here by the stairs," he told her, and pushed her firmly back through the door.

Asir started slowly toward the room where Big Joe waited. Beyond the room he could see another door, and the monster's job was apparently to keep intruders back from the inner vaults where, according to the ritual chants, the Blaze of the Winds could be kindled.

Halfway along the corridor, the voice called out again, beginning a kind of sing-song chant: "*Big Joe will kill you, Big Joe will kill you, Big Joe will kill you—*"

He turned slowly, searching for the speaker. But the voice seemed to come from a black disk on the wall. The talking-machines perhaps, as mentioned somewhere in the ritual.

A few paces from the entrance to the room, the voice fell silent. He stopped at the door, staring in at the monster. Then he took a deep breath and began chanting the twenty-four numbers in a loud but quavering voice. Big Joe remained in his motionless crouch. Nothing happened. He stepped through the doorway.

*

Big Joe emitted a deafening roar, straightened with a metallic groan, and lumbered toward him, taloned hands extended and eyes blazing furiously. Asir shrieked and ran for his life.

Then he saw Mara lying sprawled in the stairway entrance. She had fainted. Blocking an impulse to leap over her and flee alone, he stopped to lift her.

But suddenly he realized that there was no pursuit. He looked back. Big Joe had returned to his former position, and he appeared to be asleep again. Puzzled, Asir stepped back into the corridor.

"If you have come to plunder, go back!"

He moved gingerly ahead again.

"Big Joe will kill you, Big Joe will kill you, Big Joe will kill—"

He recovered the barbed pike from the floor and stole into the zone of silence. This time he stopped to look around. Slowly he reached the pike-staff through the doorway. Nothing happened. He stepped closer and waved it around inside. Big Joe remained motionless.

Then he dropped the point of the pike to the floor. The monster bellowed and started to rise. Asir leaped back, scalp crawling. But Big Joe settled back in his crouch.

Fighting a desire to flee, Asir reached the pike through the door and rapped it on the floor again. This time nothing happened. He glanced down. The pike's point rested in the center of a gray floor-tile, just to the left of the entrance. The floor was a checkerboard pattern of gray and white. He tapped another gray square, and this time the monster started out of his drowse again.

After a moment's thought, he began touching each tile within reach of the door. Most of them brought a response from Big Joe. He found four that did not. He knelt down before the door to peer at them closely. The first was unmarked. The second bore a dot in the center. The third bore two, and the fourth three—in order of their distance from the door.

He stood up and stepped inside again, standing on the first tile. Big Joe remained motionless. He stepped diagonally left to the second—straight ahead to the third—then diagonally right to the fourth. He stood there for a moment, trembling and staring at the Sleeper. He was four feet past the door!

Having assured himself that the monster was still asleep, he crouched to peer at the next tiles. He stared for a long time, but found no similar markings. Were the dots coincidence?

19

He reached out with the pike, then drew it back. He was too close to the Sleeper to risk a mistake. He stood up and looked around carefully, noting each detail of the room—and of the floor in particular. He counted the rows and columns of tiles—twenty-four each way.

Twenty-four—and there were twenty-four numbers in the series that was somehow connected with safe passage through the room. He frowned and muttered through the series to himself—0,1,2,3,3,3,2,2, 1....

The first four numbers—0,1,2,3. And the tiles—the first with no dots, the second with one, the third with two, the fourth with three. But the four tiles were not in a straight line, and there were no marked ones beyond the fourth. He backed out of the room and studied them from the end of the corridor again.

Mara had come dizzily awake and was calling for him weakly. He replied reassuringly and turned to his task again. "First tile, then diagonally left, then straight, then diagonally right—"

0, 1, 2, 3, 3.

A hunch came. He advanced as far as the second tile, then reached as far ahead as he could and touched the square diagonally right from the fourth one. Big Joe remained motionless but began to speak. His scalp bristled at the growling voice.

"*If the intruder makes an error, Big Joe will kill.*"

Standing tense, ready to leap back to the corridor, he touched the square again. The motionless behemoth repeated the grim warning.

Asir tried to reach the square diagonally right from the fifth, but could not without stepping up to the third. Taking a deep breath, he stepped up and extended the pike cautiously, keeping his eyes on Big Joe. The pike rapped the floor.

"*If the intruder makes an error, Big Joe will kill.*"

But the huge figure remained in his place.

*

Starting from the first square, the path went left, straight, right, right, right. And after zero, the numbers went 1, 2, 3, 3, 3. Apparently he had found the key. One meant a square to the southeast; two meant south; and three southwest. Shivering, he moved up to the fifth square upon which the monster growled his first warning. He looked back at the door, then at Big Joe. The taloned hands could grab him before he could dive back into the corridor.

He hesitated. He could either turn back now, or gamble his life on the accuracy of the tentative belief. The girl was calling to him again.

"Come to the end of the corridor!" he replied.

She came hurriedly, to his surprise.

"*No!*" he bellowed. "Stay back of the entrance! Not on the tile! *No!*"

Slowly she withdrew the foot that hung poised over a trigger-tile.

"You can't come in unless you know how," he gasped.

She blinked at him and glanced nervously back over her shoulder. "But I hear them. They're coming down the stairs."

Asir cursed softly. Now he *had* to go ahead.

"Wait just a minute," he said. "Then I'll show you how to come through."

He advanced to the last tile that he had tested and stopped. The next two numbers were two—for straight ahead. And they would take him within easy reach of the long taloned arms of the murderous sentinel. He glanced around in fright at the crushed bones scattered across the floor. Some were human. Others were animal-sacrifices tossed in by the priests.

He had tested only one two—back near the door. If he made a mistake, he would never escape; no need bothering with the pike.

He stepped to the next tile and closed his eyes.

"*If the intruder makes an error, Big Joe will kill.*"

He opened his eyes again and heaved a breath of relief.

"Asir! They're getting closer! I can hear them!"

He listened for a moment. A faint murmur of angry voices in the distance. "All right," he said calmly. "Step only on the tiles I tell you. See the gray one at the left of the door?"

She pointed. "This one?"

"Yes, step on it."

The girl moved up and stared fearfully at the monstrous sentinel. He guided her up toward him. "Diagonally left—one ahead—diagonally right. Now don't be frightened when he speaks—"

The girl came on until she stood one square behind him. Her quick frightened breathing blended with the growing sounds of shouting from the stairway. He glanced up at Big Joe, noticing for the first time that the steel jaws were stained with a red-brown crust. He shuddered.

The grim chess-game continued a cautious step at a time, with the girl following one square behind him. What if she fainted again? And fell across a triggered tile? They passed within a foot of Big Joe's arm.

Looking up, he saw the monster's eyes move—following them, scrutinizing them as they passed. He froze.

"We want no plunder," he said to the machine.

The gaze was steady and unwinking.

"The air is leaking away from the world."

The monster remained silent.

"Hurry!" whimpered the girl. Their pursuers were gaining rapidly and they had crossed only half the distance to the opposing doorway. Progress was slower now, for Asir needed occasionally to repeat through the whole series of numbers, looking back to count squares and make certain that the next step was not a fatal one.

"They won't dare to come in after us," he said hopefully.

"And if they do?"

"*If the intruder makes an error, Big Joe will kill,*" announced the machine as Asir took another step.

"Eight squares to go!" he muttered, and stopped to count again.

"Asir! They're in the corridor!"

Hearing the rumble of voices, he looked back to see blue-robed men spilling out of the stairway and milling down the corridor toward the room. But halfway down the hall, the priests paused—seeing the unbelievable: two intruders walking safely past their devil-god. They growled excitedly among themselves. Asir took another step. Again the machine voiced the monotonous warning.

"*If the intruder makes an error....*"

*

Hearing their deity speak, the priests of Big Joe babbled wildly and withdrew a little. But one, more impulsive than the rest, began shrieking.

"*Kill the intruders! Cut them down with your spears!*"

Asir glanced back to see two of them racing toward the room, lances cocked for the throw. If a spear struck a trigger-tile—

"Stop!" he bellowed, facing around.

The two priests paused. Wondering if it would result in his sudden death, he rested a hand lightly against the huge steel arm of the robot, then leaned against it. The huge eyes were staring down at him, but Big Joe did not move.

The spearmen stood frozen, gaping at the thief's familiarity with the horrendous hulk. Then, slowly they backed away.

Continuing his bluff, he looked up at Big Joe and spoke in a loud voice. "If they throw their spears or try to enter, kill them."

He turned his back on the throng in the hall and continued the cautious advance. Five to go, four, three, two—

He paused to stare into the room beyond. Gleaming machinery—all silent—and great panels, covered with a multitude of white circles and dials. His heart sank. If here lay the magic that controlled the Blaze of the Great Wind, he could never hope to rekindle it.

He stepped through the doorway, and the girl followed. Immediately the robot spoke like low thunder.

"*The identity of the two technologists is recognized. Hereafter they may pass with impunity. Big Joe is charged to ask the following: why do the technologists come, when it is not yet time?*"

Staring back, Asir saw that the robot's head had turned so that he was looking directly back at the thief and the girl. Asir also saw that someone had approached the door again. Not priests, but townspeople.

IT TAKES A THIEF

He stared, recognizing the Chief Commoner, and the girl's father Welkir, three other Senior Kinsmen, and—Slubil, the executioner who had nailed him to the post.

"Father! Stay back."

Welkir remained silent, glaring at them. He turned and whispered to the Chief Commoner. The Chief Commoner whispered to Slubil. The executioner nodded grimly and took a short-axe from his belt thong. He stepped through the entrance, his left foot striking the zero-tile. He peered at Big Joe and saw that the monster remained motionless. He grinned at the ones behind him, then snarled in Asir's direction.

"Your sentence has been changed, thief."

"Don't try to cross, Slubil!" Asir barked.

Slubil spat, brandished the axe, and stalked forward. Big Joe came up like a resurrection of fury, and his bellow was explosive in the vaults. Slubil froze, then stupidly drew back his axe.

Asir gasped as the talons closed. He turned away quickly. Slubil's scream was cut off abruptly by a ripping sound, then a series of dull cracks and snaps. The girl shrieked and closed her eyes. There were two distinct thuds as Big Joe tossed Slubil aside.

The priests and the townspeople—all except Welkir—had fled from the corridor and up the stairway. Welkir was on his knees, his hands covering his face.

"Mara!" he moaned. "My daughter."

"Go back, Father," she called.

Dazed, the old man picked himself up weakly and staggered down the corridor toward the stairway. When he passed the place of the first warning voice, the robot moved again—arose slowly and turned toward Asir and Mara who backed quickly away, deeper into the room of strange machines. Big Joe came lumbering slowly after them.

Asir looked around for a place to flee, but the monster stopped in the doorway. He spoke again, a mechanical drone like memorised ritual.

"Big Joe is charged with announcing his function for the intelligence of the technologists. His primary function is to prevent the entrance of possibly destructive organisms into the vaults containing the control equipment for the fusion reaction which must periodically renew atmospheric oxygen. His secondary function is to direct the technologists to records containing such information as they may need. His tertiary function is to carry out simple directions given by the technologists if such directions are possible to his limited design."

Asir stared at the lumbering creature and realized for the first time that it was not alive, but only a machine built by the ancients to perform specific tasks. Despite the fresh redness about his hands and jaws, Big Joe was no more guilty of Slubil's death than a grinding mill would be if the squat sadist had climbed into it while the Marsoxen were yoked to the crushing roller.

Perhaps the ancients had been unnecessarily brutal in building such a guard—but at least they had built him to *look* like a destroyer, and to give ample warning to the intruder. Glancing around at the machinery, he vaguely understood the reason for Big Joe. Such metals as these would mean riches for swordmakers and smiths and plunderers of all kinds.

*

Asir straightened his shoulders and addressed the machine.

"Teach us how to kindle the Blaze of the Great Wind."

"Teaching is not within the designed functions of Big Joe. I am charged to say: the renewal reaction should not be begun before the Marsyear 6,000, as the builders reckoned time."

Asir frowned. The years were no longer numbered, but only named in honor of the Chief Commoners who ruled the villages. "How long until the year 6,000?" he asked.

Big Joe clucked like an adding machine. "Twelve Marsyears, technologist."

Asir stared at the complicated machinery. Could they learn to operate it in twelve years? It seemed impossible.

"How can we begin to learn?" he asked the robot.

"This is an instruction room, where you may examine records. The control mechanisms are installed in the deepest vault."

IT TAKES A THIEF

Asir frowned and walked to the far end of the hall where another door opened into—*another anteroom, with another Big Joe!* As he approached the second robot spoke:

"If the intruder has not acquired the proper knowledge, Big Oswald will kill."

Thunderstruck, he leaped back from the entrance and swayed heavily against an instrument panel. The panel lit up and a polite recorded voice began reading something about "President Snell's role in the Eighth World War". He lurched away from the panel and stumbled back toward Mara who sat glumly on the foundation slab of a weighty machine.

"What are you laughing about?" she muttered.

"We're still in the first grade!" he groaned, envisioning a sequence of rooms. "We'll have to learn the magic of the ancients before we pass to the next."

"The ancients weren't so great," she grumbled. "Look at the mural on the wall."

Asir looked, and saw only a strange design of circles about a bright splash of yellow that might have been the sun. "What about it?" he asked.

"My father taught me about the planets," she said. "That is supposed to be the way they go around the sun."

"What's wrong with it?"

"One planet too many," she said. "Everyone knows that there is only an asteroid belt between Mars and Venus. The picture shows a planet there."

Asir shrugged indifferently, being interested only in the machinery. "Can't you allow them one small mistake?"

"I suppose." She paused, gazing miserably in the direction in which her father had gone. "What do we do now?"

Asir considered it for a long time. Then he spoke to Big Joe. "You will come with us to the village."

The machine was silent for a moment, then: *"There is an apparent contradiction between primary and tertiary functions. Request priority decision by technologist."*

Asir failed to understand. He repeated his request. The robot turned slowly and stepped through the doorway. He waited.

Asir grinned. "Let's go back up," he said to the girl.

She arose eagerly. They crossed the anteroom to the corridor and began the long climb toward the surface, with Big Joe lumbering along behind.

"What about your banishment, Asir?" she asked gravely.

"Wait and see." He envisioned the pandemonium that would reign when girl, man, and robot marched through the village to the council house, and he chuckled. "I think that I shall be the next Chief Commoner," he said. "And my councilmen will all be thieves."

"Thieves!" she gasped. "Why?"

"Thieves who are not afraid to steal the knowledge of the gods—and become technologists, to kindle the Blaze of the Winds."

"What is a 'technologist', Asir?" she asked worshipfully.

Asir glowered at himself for blundering with words he did not understand, but could not admit ignorance to Mara who clung tightly to his arm. "I think," he said, "that a technologist is a thief who tells the gods what to do."

"Kiss me, Technologist," she told him in a small voice.

Big Joe clanked to a stop to wait for them to move on. He waited a long time.